'EVERYTHING
WAS DEAD,
EVERYTHING
UNREAL; THE
DARK MOB
WAS MADE
UP OF STIFF
LAY-FIGURES.'

JOHN STEINBECK
Born 1902, Salinas, California, USA
Died 1968, New York City, USA

The stories in this volume are taken from *The Long Valley*,
first published in 1938.

STEINBECK IN PENGUIN MODERN CLASSICS

JOHN STEINBECK

The Vigilante

PENGUIN BOOKS

PENGUIN CLASSICS

UK | USA | Canada | Ireland | Australia
India | New Zealand | South Africa

Penguin Books is part of the Penguin Random House group
of companies whose addresses can be found at
global.penguinrandomhouse.com.

Penguin
Random House
UK

This selection first published 2018
001

Set in 12/15 pt Dante MT Std
Typeset by Jouve (UK), Milton Keynes
Printed in Great Britain by Clays Ltd, St Ives plc

ISBN: 978–0–241–33895–7

www.greenpenguin.co.uk

MIX
Paper from
responsible sources
FSC
www.fsc.org   FSC® C018179

Penguin Random House is committed to a
sustainable future for our business, our readers
and our planet. This book is made from Forest
Stewardship Council® certified paper.

Contents

The Vigilante

The great surge of emotion, the milling and shouting of the people fell gradually to silence in the town park. A crowd of people still stood under the elm trees, vaguely lighted by a blue street light two blocks away. A tired quiet settled on the people; some members of the mob began to sneak away into the darkness. The park lawn was cut to pieces by the feet of the crowd.

Mike knew it was all over. He could feel the letdown in himself. He was as heavily weary as though he had gone without sleep for several nights, but it was a dream-like weariness, a grey comfortable weariness. He pulled his cap down over his eyes and moved away, but before leaving the park he turned for one last look.

In the center of the mob someone had lighted a twisted newspaper and was holding it up. Mike could see how the flame curled about the feet of the grey naked body hanging from the elm tree. It seemed curious to him that negroes turn a bluish grey when they are dead. The burning newspaper lighted the heads of the up-looking men, silent men and fixed; they didn't move their eyes from the hanged man.

Mike felt a little irritation at whoever it was who was trying to burn the body. He turned to a man who stood beside him in the near-darkness. 'That don't do no good,' he said.

The man moved away without replying.

The newspaper torch went out, leaving the park almost black by contrast. But immediately another twisted paper was lighted and held up against the feet. Mike moved to another watching man. 'That don't do no good,' he repeated. 'He's dead now. They can't hurt him none.'

The second man grunted but did not look away from the flaming paper. 'It's a good job,' he said. 'This'll save the country a lot of money and no sneaky lawyers getting in.'

'That's what I say,' Mike agreed. 'No sneaky lawyers. But it don't do no good to try to burn him.'

The man continued staring toward the flame. 'Well, it can't do much harm, either.'

Mike filled his eyes with the scene. He felt that he was dull. He wasn't seeing enough of it. Here was a thing he would want to remember later so he could tell about it, but the dull tiredness seemed to cut the sharpness off the picture. His brain told him this was a terrible and important affair, but his eyes and his feelings didn't agree. It was just ordinary. Half an hour before, when he had been howling with the mob and fighting for a chance to help pull on the rope, then his chest had been so full that he had found he was crying. But now everything was dead, everything unreal; the dark mob was made up of stiff lay-figures. In the flamelight the faces were as expressionless as wood. Mike felt the stiffness, the unreality in himself, too. He turned away at last and walked out of the park.

The moment he left the outskirts of the mob a cold loneliness fell upon him. He walked quickly along the street wishing that some other man might be walking beside him. The wide street was deserted, empty, as unreal as the park had been. The two steel lines of the car tracks stretched glimmering away down the street under the electroliers, and the dark store windows reflected the midnight globes.

A gentle pain began to make itself felt in Mike's chest. He felt with his fingers; the muscles were sore. Then he remembered. He was in the front line of the mob when it rushed the closed jail door. A driving line forty men deep had crushed Mike against the door like the head of a ram. He had hardly felt it then, and even now the pain seemed to have the dull quality of loneliness.

Two blocks ahead the burning neon word BEER hung over the sidewalk. Mike hurried toward it. He hoped there would be people there, and talk, to remove this silence; and he hoped the men wouldn't have been to the lynching.

The bartender was alone in his little bar, a small, middle-aged man with a melancholy moustache and an expression like an aged mouse, wise and unkempt and fearful.

He nodded quickly as Mike came in. 'You look like you been walking in your sleep,' he said.

Mike regarded him with wonder. 'That's just how I feel, too, like I been walking in my sleep.'

'Well, I can give you a shot if you want.'

Mike hesitated. 'No – I'm kind of thirsty. I'll take a beer . . . Was you there?'

The little man nodded his mouse-like head again. 'Right at the last, after he was all up and it was all over. I figured a lot of the fellas would be thirsty, so I came back and opened up. Nobody but you so far. Maybe I was wrong.'

'They might be along later,' said Mike. 'There's a lot of them still in the park. They cooled off, though. Some of them trying to burn him with newspapers. That don't do no good.'

'Not a bit of good,' said the little bartender. He twitched his thin moustache.

Mike knocked a few grains of celery salt into his beer and took a long drink. 'That's good,' he said. 'I'm kind of dragged out.'

The bartender leaned close to him over the bar, his eyes were bright. 'Was you there all the time – to the jail and everything?'

Mike drank again and then looked through his beer and watched the beads of bubbles rising from the grains of salt in the bottom of the glass. 'Everything,' he said. 'I was one of the first in the jail, and I helped pull on the rope. There's times when citizens got to take the law in their own hands. Sneaky lawyer comes along and gets some fiend out of it.'

The mousy head jerked up and down. 'You God-dam' right,' he said. 'Lawyers can get them out of anything. I guess the nigger was guilty all right.'

'Oh, sure! Somebody said he even confessed.'

The head came close over the bar again. 'How did it start, mister? I was only there after it was all over, and then I only stayed a minute and then came back to open up in case any of the fellas might want a glass of beer.'

Mike drained his glass and pushed it out to be filled. 'Well, of course everybody knew it was going to happen. I was in a bar across from the jail. Been there all afternoon. A guy came in and says, "What are we waiting for?" So we went across the street, and a lot more guys was there and a lot more come. We all stood there and yelled. Then the sheriff come out and made a speech, but we yelled him down. A guy with a twenty-two rifle went along the street and shot out the street lights. Well, then we rushed the jail doors and bust them. The sheriff wasn't going to do nothing. It wouldn't do him no good to shoot a lot of honest men to save a nigger fiend.'

'And election coming on, too,' the bartender put in.

'Well, the sheriff started yelling, "Get the right man, boys, for Christ's sake get the right man. He's in the fourth cell down."

'It was kind of pitiful,' Mike said slowly. 'The other prisoners were so scared. We could see them through the bars. I never seen such faces.'

The bartender excitedly poured himself a small glass of whiskey and poured it down. 'Can't blame 'em much. Suppose you was in for thirty days and a lynch mob came through. You'd be scared they'd get the wrong man.'

'That's what I say. It was kind of pitiful. Well, we got to the nigger's cell. He just stood stiff with his eyes closed like he was dead drunk. One of the guys slugged him down and he got up, and then somebody else socked him and he went over and hit his head on the cement floor.' Mike leaned over the bar and tapped the polished wood with his forefinger. ' 'Course this is only my idea, but I think that killed him. Because I helped get his clothes off, and he never made a wiggle, and when we strung him up he didn't jerk around none. No, sir. I think he was dead all the time, after that second guy smacked him.'

'Well, it's all the same in the end.'

'No, it ain't. You like to do the thing right. He had it coming to him, and he should have got it.' Mike reached into his trousers pocket and brought out a piece of torn blue denim. 'That's a piece of the pants he had on.'

The bartender bent close and inspected the cloth. He jerked his head up at Mike. 'I'll give you a buck for it.'

'Oh no, you won't!'

'All right. I'll give you two bucks for half of it.'

Mike looked suspiciously at him. 'What you want it for?'

'Here! Give me your glass! Have a beer on me. I'll pin it up on the wall with a little card under it. The fellas that come in will like to look at it.'

Mike haggled the piece of cloth in two with his pocket knife and accepted two silver dollars from the bartender.

'I know a show card writer,' the little man said. 'Comes in every day. He'll print me up a nice little card to go under it.' He looked wary. 'Think the sheriff will arrest anybody?'

' 'Course not. What's he want to start any trouble for? There was a lot of votes in that crowd tonight.

Soon as they all go away, the sheriff will come and cut the nigger down and clean up some.'

The bartender looked toward the door. 'I guess I was wrong about the fellas wanting a drink. It's getting late.'

'I guess I'll get along home. I feel tired.'

'If you go south, I'll close up and walk a ways with you. I live on south Eighth.'

'Why, that's only two blocks from my house. I live on south Sixth. You must go right past my house. Funny I never saw you around.'

The bartender washed Mike's glass and took off the long apron. He put on his hat and coat, walked to the door and switched off the red neon sign and the house lights. For a moment the two men stood on the sidewalk looking back toward the park. The city was silent. There was no sound from the park. A policeman walked along a block away, turning his flash into the store windows.

'You see?' said Mike. 'Just like nothing happened.'

'Well, if the fellas wanted a glass of beer they must have gone someplace else.'

'That's what I told you,' said Mike.

They swung along the empty street and turned

south, out of the business district. 'My name's Welch,' the bartender said. 'I only been in this town about two years.'

The loneliness had fallen on Mike again. 'It's funny –' he said, and then, 'I was born right in this town, right in the house I live in now. I got a wife but no kids. Both of us born right in this town. Everybody knows us.'

They walked on for a few blocks. The stores dropped behind and the nice houses with bushy gardens and cut lawns lined the street. The tall shade trees were shadowed on the sidewalk by the street lights. Two night dogs went slowly by, smelling at each other.

Welch said softly – 'I wonder what kind of a fella he was – the nigger, I mean.'

Mike answered out of his loneliness. 'The papers all said he was a fiend. I read all the papers. That's what they all said.'

'Yes, I read them, too. But it makes you wonder about him. I've known some pretty nice niggers.'

Mike turned his head and spoke protestingly. 'Well, I've knew some dam' fine niggers myself. I've worked right 'longside some niggers and they was

as nice as any white man you could want to meet. –
But not no fiends.'

His vehemence silenced little Welch for a moment. Then he said, 'You couldn't tell, I guess, what
kind of a fella he was?'

'No – he just stood there stiff, with his mouth shut
and his eyes tight closed and his hands right down at
his sides. And then one of the guys smacked him. It's
my idea he was dead when we took him out.'

Welch sidled close on the walk. 'Nice gardens
along here. Must take a lot of money to keep them
up.' He walked even closer, so that his shoulder
touched Mike's arm. 'I never been to a lynching.
How's it make you feel – afterwards?'

Mike shied away from the contact. 'It don't make
you feel nothing.' He put down his head and in-
creased his pace. The little bartender had nearly to
trot to keep up. The street lights were fewer. It was
darker and safer. Mike burst out, 'Makes you feel
kind of cut off and tired, but kind of satisfied, too.
Like you done a good job – but tired and kind of
sleepy.' He slowed his steps. 'Look, there's a light in
the kitchen. That's where I live. My old lady's waiting up for me.' He stopped in front of his little house.

Welch stood nervously beside him. 'Come into my place when you want a glass of beer – or a shot. Open till midnight. I treat my friends right.' He scampered away like an aged mouse.

Mike called, 'Goodnight.'

He walked around the side of his house and went in the back door. His thin, petulant wife was sitting by the open gas oven warming herself. She turned complaining eyes on Mike where he stood in the doorway.

Then her eyes widened and hung on his face. 'You been with a woman,' she said hoarsely. 'What woman you been with?'

Mike laughed. 'You think you're pretty slick, don't you? You're a slick one, ain't you? What makes you think I been with a woman?'

She said fiercely, 'You think I can't tell by the look on your face that you been with a woman?'

'All right,' said Mike. 'If you're so slick and know-it-all, I won't tell you nothing. You can just wait for the morning paper.'

He saw doubt come into the dissatisfied eyes. 'Was it the nigger?' she asked. 'Did they get the nigger? Everybody said they was going to.'

'Find out for yourself if you're so slick. I ain't going to tell you nothing.'

He walked through the kitchen and went into the bathroom. A little mirror hung on the wall. Mike took off his cap and looked at his face. 'By God, she was right,' he thought. 'That's just exactly how I do feel.'

The Snake

It was almost dark when young Dr Phillips swung his sack to his shoulder and left the tide pool. He climbed up over the rocks and squashed along the street in his rubber boots. The street lights were on by the time he arrived at his little commercial laboratory on the cannery street of Monterey. It was a tight little building, standing partly on piers over the bay water and partly on the land. On both sides the big corrugated-iron sardine canneries crowded in on it.

Dr Phillips climbed the wooden steps and opened the door. The white rats in their cages scampered up and down the wire, and the captive cats in their pens mewed for milk. Dr Phillips turned on the glaring light over the dissection table and dumped his clammy sack on the floor. He walked to the glass cages by the window where the rattlesnakes lived, leaned over and looked in.

The snakes were bunched and resting in the corners of the cage, but every head was clear; the dusty eyes seemed to look at nothing, but as the young man leaned over the cage the forked tongues, black on the ends and pink behind, twittered out and waved slowly up and down. Then the snakes recognized the man and pulled in their tongues.

Dr Phillips threw off his leather coat and built a fire in the tin stove; he set a kettle of water on the stove and dropped a can of beans into the water. Then he stood staring down at the sack on the floor. He was a slight young man with the mild, preoccupied eyes of one who looks through a microscope a great deal. He wore a short blond beard.

The draft ran breathily up the chimney and a glow of warmth came from the stove. The little waves washed quietly about the piles under the building. Arranged on shelves about the room were tier above tier of museum jars containing the mounted marine specimens the laboratory dealt in.

Dr Phillips opened a side door and went into his bedroom, a book-lined cell containing an army cot, a reading light and an uncomfortable wooden chair. He pulled off his rubber boots and put on a pair of sheepskin slippers. When he went back to the other room the water in the kettle was already beginning to hum.

He lifted his sack to the table under the white light and emptied out two dozen common starfish. These he laid out side by side on the table. His preoccupied eyes turned to the busy rats in the wire cages. Taking grain from a paper sack, he poured it into the feeding troughs. Instantly the rats scrambled down from the wire and fell upon the food. A bottle of milk stood on a glass shelf between a small mounted octopus and a jellyfish. Dr Phillips lifted down the milk and walked to the cat cage, but before he filled the containers he reached in the cage and gently picked out a big rangy alley tabby. He stroked her for a moment and then dropped her in a small black painted box, closed the lid and bolted it and then turned on a petcock which admitted gas into the killing chamber. While the short soft struggle went on in the black box he filled the saucers with milk. One of the cats arched against his hand and he smiled and petted her neck.

The box was quiet now. He turned off the petcock, for the airtight box would be full of gas.

On the stove the pan of water was bubbling furiously about the can of beans. Dr Phillips lifted out the can with a big pair of forceps, opened it, and emptied the beans into a glass dish. While he ate he watched the starfish on the table. From between the rays little drops of milky fluid were exuding. He bolted his beans and when they were gone he put the dish in the sink and stepped to the equipment cupboard. From this he took a microscope and a pile of little glass dishes. He filled the dishes one by one with sea water from a tap and arranged them in a line beside the starfish. He took out his watch and laid it on the table under the pouring white light. The waves washed with little sighs against the piles under the floor. He took an eyedropper from a drawer and bent over the starfish.

At that moment there were quick soft steps on the wooden stairs and a strong knocking at the door. A slight grimace of annoyance crossed the young man's face as he went to open. A tall, lean woman stood in the doorway. She was dressed in a severe dark suit – her straight black hair, growing low on a flat forehead, was mussed as though the wind had been blowing it. Her black eyes glittered in the strong light.

She spoke in a soft throaty voice, 'May I come in? I want to talk to you.'

'I'm very busy just now,' he said half-heartedly. 'I have to do things at times.' But he stood away from the door. The tall woman slipped in.

'I'll be quiet until you can talk to me.'

He closed the door and brought the uncomfortable chair from the bedroom. 'You see,' he apologized, 'the process is started and I must get to it.' So many people wandered in and asked questions. He had little routines of explanations for the commoner processes. He could say them without thinking. 'Sit here. In a few minutes I'll be able to listen to you.'

The tall woman leaned over the table. With the eyedropper the young man gathered fluid from between the rays of the starfish and squirted it into a bowl of water, and then he drew some milky fluid and squirted it in the same bowl and stirred the water gently with the eyedropper. He began his little patter of explanation.

'When starfish are sexually mature they release sperm and ova when they are exposed at low tide. By choosing mature specimens and taking them out of the water, I give them a condition of low tide. Now I've mixed the sperm and eggs. Now I put some of the mixture in each one of these ten watch glasses. In ten minutes I will kill those in the first glass with menthol, twenty minutes later I will kill the second group and then a new group every twenty minutes. Then I will have arrested the process in stages, and I will mount the series on microscope slides for bio-logic study.' He paused. 'Would you like to look at this first group under the microscope?'

'No, thank you.'

He turned quickly to her. People always wanted to look through the glass. She was not looking at the table at all, but at him. Her black eyes were on him, but they did not seem to see him. He realized why – the irises were as dark as the pupils, there was no color line between the two. Dr Phillips was piqued at her answer. Although answering questions bored him, a lack of interest in what he was doing irritated him. A desire to arouse her grew in him.

'While I'm waiting the first ten minutes I have something to do. Some people don't like to see it. Maybe you'd better step into that room until I finish.'

'No,' she said in her soft flat tone. 'Do what you wish. I will wait until you can talk to me.' Her hands rested side by side on her lap. She was completely at rest. Her eyes were bright but the rest of her was almost in a state of suspended animation. He thought, 'Low metabolic rate, almost as low as a frog's, from the looks.' The desire to shock her out of her inanition possessed him again.

He brought a little wooden cradle to the table, laid out scalpels and scissors and rigged a big hollow needle to a pressure tube. Then from the killing chamber he brought the limp dead cat and laid it in the cradle and tied its legs to hooks in the sides. He glanced sidewise at the woman. She had not moved. She was still at rest.

The cat grinned up into the light, its pink tongue stuck out between its needle teeth. Dr Phillips deftly snipped open the skin at the throat; with a scalpel he slit through and found an artery. With flawless technique he put the needle in the vessel and tied it in with gut. 'Embalming fluid,' he explained. 'Later I'll inject yellow mass into the veinous system and red mass into the arterial system – for bloodstream dissection – biology classes.'

He looked around at her again. Her dark eyes seemed veiled with dust. She looked without expression at the cat's open throat. Not a drop of blood had escaped. The incision was clean. Dr Phillips looked at his watch. 'Time for the first group.' He shook a few crystals of menthol into the first watch glass.

The woman was making him nervous. The rats climbed about on the wire of their cage again and squeaked softly. The waves under the building beat with little shocks on the piles.

The young man shivered. He put a few lumps of coal in the stove and sat down. 'Now,' he said. 'I haven't anything to do for twenty minutes.' He noticed how short her chin was between lower lip and point. She seemed to awaken slowly, to come up out of some deep pool of consciousness. Her head raised and her dark dusty eyes moved about the room and then came back to him.

'I was waiting,' she said. Her hands remained side by side on her lap. 'You have snakes?'

'Why, yes,' he said rather loudly. 'I have about two dozen rattlesnakes. I milk out the venom and send it to the anti-venom laboratories.'

She continued to look at him but her eyes did not center on him, rather they covered him and seemed to see in a big circle all around him. 'Have you a male snake, a male rattlesnake?'

'Well, it just happens I know I have. I came in one morning and found a big snake in – in coition with a smaller one. That's very rare in captivity. You see, I do know I have a male snake.'

'Where is he?'

'Why, right in the glass cage by the window there.'

Her head swung slowly around but her two quiet hands did not move. She turned back toward him. 'May I see?'

He got up and walked to the case by the window. On the sand bottom the knot of rattlesnakes lay entwined, but their heads were clear. The tongues came out and flickered a moment and then waved up and down feeling the air for vibrations. Dr Phillips nervously turned his head. The woman was standing beside him. He had not heard her get up from the chair. He had heard only the splash of water among the piles and the scampering of the rats on the wire screen.

She said softly, 'Which is the male you spoke of?'

He pointed to a thick, dusty grey snake lying by itself in one corner of the cage. 'That one. He's nearly five feet long. He comes from Texas. Our Pacific coast snakes are usually smaller. He's been taking all the rats, too. When I want the others to eat I have to take him out.'

The woman stared down at the blunt dry head. The forked tongue slipped out and hung quivering for a long moment. 'And you're sure he's a male.'

'Rattlesnakes are funny,' he said glibly. 'Nearly every generalization proves wrong. I don't like to say anything definite about rattlesnakes, but – yes – I can assure you he's a male.'

Her eyes did not move from the flat head. 'Will you sell him to me?'

'Sell him?' he cried. 'Sell him to you?'

'You do sell specimens, don't you?'

'Oh – yes. Of course I do. Of course I do.'

'How much? Five dollars? Ten?'

'Oh! Not more than five. But – do you know anything about rattlesnakes? You might be bitten.'

She looked at him for a moment. 'I don't intend to take him. I want to leave him here, but – I want him to be mine. I want to come here and look at him and feed him and to know he's mine.' She opened a little purse and took out a five-dollar bill. 'Here! Now he is mine.'

Dr Phillips began to be afraid. 'You could come to look at him without owning him.'

'I want him to be mine.'

'Oh, Lord!' he cried. 'I've forgotten the time.' He ran to the table. 'Three minutes over. It won't matter much.' He shook menthol crystals into the second watch glass. And then he was drawn back to the cage where the woman still stared at the snake.

She asked, 'What does he eat?'

'I feed them white rats, rats from the cage over there.'

'Will you put him in the other cage? I want to feed him.'

'But he doesn't need food. He's had a rat already this week. Sometimes they don't eat for three or four months. I had one that didn't eat for over a year.'

In her low monotone she asked, 'Will you sell me a rat?'

He shrugged his shoulders. 'I see. You want to watch how rattlesnakes eat. All right. I'll show you. The rat will cost twenty-five cents. It's better than a bullfight if you look at it one way, and it's simply a snake eating his dinner if you look at it another.' His tone had become acid. He hated people who made sport of natural processes. He was not a sportsman but a biologist. He could kill a thousand animals for knowledge, but not an insect for pleasure. He'd been over this in his mind before.

She turned her head slowly toward him and the beginning of a smile formed on her thin lips. 'I want to feed my snake,' she said. 'I'll put him in the other cage.' She had opened the top of the cage and dipped her hand in before he knew what she was doing. He leaped forward and pulled her back. The lid banged shut.

'Haven't you any sense,' he asked fiercely. 'Maybe he wouldn't kill you, but he'd make you damned sick in spite of what I could do for you.'

'You put him in the other cage then,' she said quietly.

Dr Phillips was shaken. He found that he was avoiding the dark eyes that didn't seem to look at anything. He felt that it was profoundly wrong to put a rat into the cage, deeply sinful; and he didn't know why. Often he had put rats in the cage when someone or other had wanted to see it, but this desire tonight sickened him. He tried to explain himself out of it.

'It's a good thing to see,' he said. 'It shows you how a snake can work. It makes you have a respect for a rattlesnake. Then, too, lots of people have dreams about the terror of snakes making the kill. I think because it is a subjective rat. The person is the rat. Once you see it the whole matter is objective. The rat is only a rat and the terror is removed.'

He took a long stick equipped with a leather noose from the wall. Opening the trap he dropped the noose over the big snake's head and tightened the thong. A piercing dry rattle filled the room. The thick body writhed and slashed about the handle of the stick as he lifted the snake out and dropped it in the feeding cage. It stood ready to strike for a time, but the buzzing gradually ceased. The snake crawled into a corner, made a big figure eight with its body and lay still.

'You see,' the young man explained, 'these snakes are quite tame. I've had them a long time. I suppose I could handle them if I wanted to, but everyone who does handle rattlesnakes gets bitten sooner or later. I just don't want to take the chance.' He glanced at the woman. He hated to put in the rat. She had moved over in front of the new cage; her black eyes were on the stony head of the snake again.

She said, 'Put in a rat.'

Reluctantly he went to the rat cage. For some reason he was sorry for the rat, and such a feeling had never come to him before. His eyes went over the mass of swarming white bodies climbing up the screen toward him. 'Which one?' he thought. 'Which one shall it be?' Suddenly he turned angrily to the woman.'Wouldn't you rather I put in a cat? Then you'd see a real fight. The cat might even win, but if it did it might kill the snake. I'll sell you a cat if you like.'

She didn't look at him. 'Put in a rat,' she said. 'I want him to eat.'

He opened the rat cage and thrust his hand in. His fingers found a tail and he lifted a plump, red-eyed rat out of the cage. It struggled up to try to bite his fingers and, failing, hung spread out and motionless from its tail. He walked quickly across the room, opened the feeding cage and dropped the rat in on the sand floor. 'Now, watch it,' he cried.

The woman did not answer him. Her eyes were on the snake where it lay still. Its tongue, flicking in and out rapidly, tasted the air of the cage.

The rat landed on its feet, turned around and sniffed at its pink naked tail and then unconcernedly trotted across the sand, smelling as it went. The room was silent. Dr Phillips did not know whether the water sighed among the piles or whether the woman sighed. Out of the corner of his eyes he saw her body crouch and stiffen.

The snake moved out smoothly, slowly. The tongue flicked in and out. The motion was so gradual, so smooth that it didn't seem to be motion at all. In the other end of the cage the rat perked up in a sitting position and began to lick down the fine white hair on its chest. The snake moved on, keeping always a deep S curve in its neck.

The silence beat on the young man. He felt the blood drifting up in his body. He said loudly, 'See! He keeps the striking curve ready. Rattlesnakes are cautious, almost cowardly animals. The mechanism is so delicate. The snake's dinner is to be got by an operation as deft as a surgeon's job. He takes no chances with his instruments.'

The snake had flowed to the middle of the cage by now. The rat looked up, saw the snake and then unconcernedly went back to licking its chest.

'It's the most beautiful thing in the world,' the young man said. His veins were throbbing. 'It's the most terrible thing in the world.'

The snake was close now. Its head lifted a few inches from the sand. The head weaved slowly back and forth, aiming, getting distance, aiming. Dr Phillips glanced again at the woman. He turned sick. She was weaving too, not much, just a suggestion.

The rat looked up and saw the snake. It dropped to four feet and back up, and then – the stroke. It was impossible to see, simply a flash. The rat jarred as though under an invisible blow. The snake backed hurriedly into the corner from which it had come, and settled down, its tongue working constantly.

'Perfect!' Dr Phillips cried. 'Right between the shoulder blades. The fangs must almost have reached the heart.'

The rat stood still, breathing like a little white

bellows. Suddenly it leaped in the air and landed on its side. Its legs kicked spasmodically for a second and it was dead.

The woman relaxed, relaxed sleepily.

'Well,' the young man demanded, 'it was an emotional bath, wasn't it?'

She turned her misty eyes to him. 'Will he eat it now?' she asked.

'Of course he'll eat it. He didn't kill it for a thrill. He killed it because he was hungry.'

The corners of the woman's mouth turned up a trifle again. She looked back at the snake. 'I want to see him eat it.'

Now the snake came out of its corner again. There was no striking curve in its neck, but it approached the rat gingerly, ready to jump back in case it attacked. It nudged the body gently with its blunt nose, and drew away. Satisfied that it was dead, the snake touched the body all over with its chin, from head to tail. It seemed to measure the body and to kiss it. Finally it opened its mouth and unhinged its jaws at the corners.

Dr Phillips put his will against his head to keep it from turning toward the woman. He thought, 'If

she's opening her mouth, I'll be sick. I'll be afraid.'
He succeeded in keeping his eyes away.

The snake fitted its jaws over the rat's head and
then with a slow peristaltic pulsing, began to engulf
the rat. The jaws gripped and the whole throat
crawled up, and the jaws gripped again.

Dr Phillips turned away and went to his work
table. 'You've made me miss one of the series,'
he said bitterly. 'The set won't be complete.' He
put one of the watch glasses under a low-power
microscope and looked at it, and then angrily he
poured the contents of all the dishes into the sink.
The waves had fallen so that only a wet whisper
came up through the floor. The young man lifted a
trapdoor at his feet and dropped the starfish down
into the black water. He paused at the cat, crucified
in the cradle and grinning comically into the light.
Its body was puffed with embalming fluid. He shut
off the pressure, withdrew the needle and tied
the vein.

'Would you like some coffee?' he asked.

'No, thank you. I shall be going pretty soon.'

He walked to her where she stood in front of the
snake cage. The rat was swallowed, all except an inch

of pink tail that stuck out of the snake's mouth like a sardonic tongue. The throat heaved again and the tail disappeared. The jaws snapped back into their sockets, and the big snake crawled heavily to the corner, made a big eight and dropped its head on the sand.

'He's asleep now,' the woman said. 'I'm going now. But I'll come back and feed my snake every little while. I'll pay for the rats. I want him to have plenty. And sometime – I'll take him away with me.' Her eyes came out of their dusty dream for a moment. 'Remember, he's mine. Don't take his poison. I want him to have it. Goodnight.' She walked swiftly to the door and went out. He heard her footsteps on the stairs, but he could not hear her walk away on the pavement.

Dr Phillips turned a chair around and sat down in front of the snake cage. He tried to comb out his thought as he looked at the torpid snake. 'I've read so much about psychological sex symbols,' he thought. 'It doesn't seem to explain. Maybe I'm too much alone. Maybe I should kill the snake. If I knew – no, I can't pray to anything.'

For weeks he expected her to return. 'I will go out and leave her alone here when she comes,' he decided. 'I won't see the damned thing again.'

She never came again. For months he looked for her when he walked about in the town. Several times he ran after some tall woman thinking it might be she. But he never saw her again – ever.

The Chrysanthemums

The high grey-flannel fog of winter closed off the Salinas Valley from the sky and from all the rest of the world. On every side it sat like a lid on the mountains and made of the great valley a closed pot. On the broad, level land floor the gang plows bit deep and left the black earth shining like metal where the shares had cut. On the foothill ranches across the Salinas River, the yellow stubble fields seemed to be bathed in pale cold sunshine, but there was no sunshine in the valley now in December. The thick willow scrub along the river flamed with sharp and positive yellow leaves.

It was a time of quiet and of waiting. The air was cold and tender. A light wind blew up from the southwest so that the farmers were mildly hopeful of a good rain before long; but fog and rain do not go together.

Across the river, on Henry Allen's foothill ranch there was little work to be done, for the hay was cut and stored and the orchards were plowed up to receive the rain deeply when it should come. The cattle on the higher slopes were becoming shaggy and rough-coated.

Elisa Allen, working in her flower garden, looked down across the yard and saw Henry, her husband, talking to two men in business suits. The three of them stood by the tractor shed, each man with one foot on the side of the little Fordson. They smoked cigarettes and studied the machine as they talked.

Elisa watched them for a moment and then went back to her work. She was thirty-five. Her face was lean and strong and her eyes were as clear as water. Her figure looked blocked and heavy in her gardening costume, a man's black hat pulled low down over her eyes, clodhopper shoes, a figured print dress almost completely covered by a big corduroy apron with four big pockets to hold the snips, the trowel and scratcher, the seeds and the knife she worked with. She wore heavy leather gloves to protect her hands while she worked.

She was cutting down the old year's chrysanthemum stalks with a pair of short and powerful scissors. She looked down toward the men by the tractor shed now and then. Her face was eager and mature and handsome; even her work with the scissors was over-eager, over-powerful. The chrysanthemum stems seemed too small and easy for her energy.

She brushed a cloud of hair out of her eyes with the back of her glove, and left a smudge of earth on her cheek in doing it. Behind her stood the neat white farmhouse with red geraniums close-banked around it as high as the windows. It was a hard-swept looking little house with hard-polished windows, and a clean mud-mat on the front steps.

Elisa cast another glance toward the tractor shed. The strangers were getting into their Ford coupé. She took off a glove and put her strong fingers down into the forest of new green chrysanthemum sprouts that were growing around the old roots. She spread the leaves and looked down among the close-growing stems. No aphids were there, no sowbugs or snails or cutworms. Her terrier fingers destroyed such pests before they could get started.

Elisa started at the sound of her husband's voice. He had come near quietly, and he leaned over the wire fence that protected her flower garden from cattle and dogs and chickens.

'At it again,' he said. 'You've got a strong new crop coming.'

Elisa straightened her back and pulled on the gardening glove again. 'Yes. They'll be strong this coming year.' In her tone and on her face there was a little smugness.

'You've got a gift with things,' Henry observed. 'Some of those yellow chrysanthemums you had this year were ten inches across. I wish you'd work out in the orchard and raise some apples that big.'

Her eyes sharpened. 'Maybe I could do it, too. I've a gift with things, all right. My mother had it. She could stick anything in the ground and make it grow. She said it was having planters' hands that knew how to do it.'

'Well, it sure works with flowers,' he said.

'Henry, who were those men you were talking to?'

'Why, sure, that's what I came to tell you. They were from the Western Meat Company. I sold those thirty head of three-year-old steers. Got nearly my own price, too.'

'Good,' she said. 'Good for you.'

'And I thought,' he continued, 'I thought how it's Saturday afternoon, and we might go into Salinas for dinner at a restaurant, and then to a picture show – to celebrate, you see.'

'Good,' she repeated. 'Oh, yes. That will be good.'

Henry put on his joking tone. 'There's fights tonight. How'd you like to go to the fights?'

'Oh, no,' she said breathlessly. 'No, I wouldn't like fights.'

'Just fooling, Elisa. We'll go to a movie. Let's see. It's two now. I'm going to take Scotty and bring down those steers from the hill. It'll take us maybe two hours. We'll go in town about five and have dinner at the Cominos Hotel. Like that?'

'Of course I'll like it. It's good to eat away from home.'

'All right, then. I'll go get up a couple of horses.'

She said, 'I'll have plenty of time to transplant some of these sets, I guess.'

She heard her husband calling Scotty down by the

barn. And a little later she saw the two men ride up the pale yellow hillside in search of the steers.

There was a little square sandy bed kept for rooting the chrysanthemums. With her trowel she turned the soil over and over, and smoothed it and patted it firm. Then she dug ten parallel trenches to receive the sets. Back at the chrysanthemum bed she pulled out the little crisp shoots, trimmed off the leaves of each one with her scissors and laid it on a small orderly pile.

A squeak of wheels and plod of hoofs came from the road. Elisa looked up. The country road ran along the dense bank of willows and cottonwoods that bordered the river, and up this road came a curious vehicle, curiously drawn. It was an old spring-wagon, with a round canvas top on it like the cover of a prairie schooner. It was drawn by an old bay horse and a little grey-and-white burro. A big stubble-bearded man sat between the cover flaps and drove the crawling team. Underneath the wagon, between the hind wheels, a lean and rangy mongrel dog walked sedately. Words were painted on the canvas, in clumsy, crooked letters. 'Pots, pans, knives, sisors, lawn mores, Fixed.' Two rows of articles, and the triumphantly definitive 'Fixed' below. The black paint had run down in little sharp points beneath each letter.

Elisa, squatting on the ground, watched to see the crazy, loose-jointed wagon pass by. But it didn't pass. It turned into the farm road in front of her house, crooked old wheels skirling and squeaking. The rangy dog darted from between the wheels and ran ahead. Instantly the two ranch shepherds flew out at him. Then all three stopped, and with stiff and quivering tails, with taut straight legs, with ambassadorial dignity, they slowly circled, sniffing daintily. The caravan pulled up to Elisa's wire fence and stopped. Now the newcomer dog, feeling outnumbered, lowered his tail and retired under the wagon with raised hackles and bared teeth.

The man on the wagon seat called out, 'That's a bad dog in a fight when he gets started.'

Elisa laughed. 'I see he is. How soon does he generally get started?'

The man caught up her laughter and echoed it heartily. 'Sometimes not for weeks and weeks,' he said. He climbed stiffly down, over the wheel. The horse and the donkey drooped like unwatered flowers.

Elisa saw that he was a very big man. Although his hair and beard were greying, he did not look old. His worn black suit was wrinkled and spotted with grease. The laughter had disappeared from his face and eyes the moment his laughing voice ceased. His eyes were dark, and they were full of the brooding that gets in the eyes of teamsters and of sailors. The calloused hands he rested on the wire fence were cracked, and every crack was a black line. He took off his battered hat.

'I'm off my general road, ma'am,' he said. 'Does this dirt road cut over across the river to the Los Angeles highway?'

Elisa stood up and shoved the thick scissors in her apron pocket. 'Well, yes, it does, but it winds around and then fords the river. I don't think your team could pull through the sand.'

He replied with some asperity, 'It might surprise you what them beasts can pull through.'

'When they get started?' she asked.

He smiled for a second. 'Yes. When they get started.'

'Well,' said Elisa, 'I think you'll save time if you go back to the Salinas road and pick up the highway there.'

He drew a big finger down the chicken wire and made it sing. 'I ain't in any hurry, ma'am. I go from Seattle to San Diego and back every year. Takes all my time. About six months each way. I aim to follow nice weather.'

Elisa took off her gloves and stuffed them in the apron pocket with the scissors. She touched the under edge of her man's hat, searching for fugitive hairs. 'That sounds like a nice kind of a way to live,' she said.

He leaned confidentially over the fence. 'Maybe you noticed the writing on my wagon. I mend pots and sharpen knives and scissors. You got any of them things to do?'

'Oh, no,' she said quickly. 'Nothing like that.' Her eyes hardened with resistance.

'Scissors is the worst thing,' he explained. 'Most people just ruin scissors trying to sharpen 'em, but I know how. I got a special tool. It's a little bobbit kind of thing, and patented. But it sure does the trick.'

'No. My scissors are all sharp.'

'All right, then. Take a pot,' he continued earnestly,

'a bent pot, or a pot with a hole. I can make it like new so you don't have to buy no new ones. That's a saving for you.'

'No,' she said shortly. 'I tell you I have nothing like that for you to do.'

His face fell to an exaggerated sadness. His voice took on a whining undertone. 'I ain't had a thing to do today. Maybe I won't have no supper tonight. You see I'm off my regular road. I know folks on the highway clear from Seattle to San Diego. They save their things for me to sharpen up because they know I do it so good and save them money.'

'I'm sorry,' Elisa said irritably. 'I haven't anything for you to do.'

His eyes left her face and fell to searching the ground. They roamed about until they came to the chrysanthemum bed where she had been working. 'What's them plants, ma'am?'

The irritation and resistance melted from Elisa's face. 'Oh, those are chrysanthemums, giant whites and yellows. I raise them every year, bigger than anybody around here.'

'Kind of a long-stemmed flower? Looks like a quick puff of colored smoke?' he asked.

'That's it. What a nice way to describe them.'

'They smell kind of nasty till you get used to them,' he said.

'It's a good bitter smell,' she retorted, 'not nasty at all.'

He changed his tone quickly. 'I like the smell myself.'

'I had ten-inch blooms this year,' she said.

The man leaned farther over the fence. 'Look. I know a lady down the road a piece, has got the nicest garden you ever seen. Got nearly every kind of flower but no chrysantheums. Last time I was mending a copper-bottom washtub for her (that's a hard job but I do it good), she said to me, "If you ever run acrost some nice chrysantheums I wish you'd try to get me a few seeds." That's what she told me.'

Elisa's eyes grew alert and eager. 'She couldn't have known much about chrysanthemums. You *can* raise them from seed, but it's much easier to root the little sprouts you see there.'

'Oh,' he said. 'I s'pose I can't take none to her, then.'

'Why yes you can,' Elisa cried. 'I can put some in damp sand, and you can carry them right along with you. They'll take root in the pot if you keep them damp. And then she can transplant them.'

'She'd sure like to have some, ma'am. You say they're nice ones?'

'Beautiful,' she said. 'Oh, beautiful.' Her eyes shone. She tore off the battered hat and shook out her dark pretty hair. 'I'll put them in a flowerpot, and you can take them right with you. Come into the yard.'

While the man came through the picket gate Elisa ran excitedly along the geranium-bordered path to the back of the house. And she returned carrying a big red flowerpot. The gloves were forgotten now. She kneeled on the ground by the starting bed and dug up the sandy soil with her fingers and scooped it into the bright new flowerpot. Then she picked up the little pile of shoots she had prepared. With her strong fingers she pressed them into the sand and tamped around them with her knuckles. The man stood over her. 'I'll tell you what to do,' she said. 'You remember so you can tell the lady.'

'Yes, I'll try to remember.'

'Well, look. These will take root in about a month. Then she must set them out, about a foot apart in

45

good rich earth like this, see?' She lifted a handful of dark soil for him to look at. 'They'll grow fast and tall. Now remember this: In July tell her to cut them down, about eight inches from the ground.'

'Before they bloom?' he asked.

'Yes, before they bloom.' Her face was tight with eagerness. 'They'll grow right up again. About the last of September the buds will start.'

She stopped and seemed perplexed. 'It's the budding that takes the most care,' she said hesitantly. 'I don't know how to tell you.' She looked deep into his eyes, searchingly. Her mouth opened a little, and she seemed to be listening. 'I'll try to tell you,' she said. 'Did you ever hear of planting hands?'

'Can't say I have, ma'am.'

'Well, I can only tell you what it feels like. It's when you're picking off the buds you don't want. Everything goes right down into your fingertips. You watch your fingers work. They do it themselves. You can feel how it is. They pick and pick the buds. They never make a mistake. They're with the plant. Do you see? Your fingers and the plant. You can feel that, right up your arm. They know. They never make a mistake. You can feel it. When you're like that you can't do anything wrong. Do you see that? Can you understand that?'

She was kneeling on the ground looking up at him. Her breast swelled passionately.

The man's eyes narrowed. He looked away self-consciously. 'Maybe I know,' he said. 'Sometimes in the night in the wagon there –'

Elisa's voice grew husky. She broke in on him, 'I've never lived as you do, but I know what you mean. When the night is dark – why, the stars are sharp-pointed, and there's quiet. Why, you rise up and up! Every pointed star gets driven into your body. It's like that. Hot and sharp and – lovely.'

Kneeling there, her hand went out toward his legs in the greasy black trousers. Her hesitant fingers almost touched the cloth. Then her hand dropped to the ground. She crouched low like a fawning dog.

He said, 'It's nice, just like you say. Only when you don't have no dinner, it ain't.'

She stood up then, very straight, and her face was ashamed. She held the flowerpot out to him and placed it gently in his arms. 'Here. Put it in your wagon, on the seat, where you can watch it. Maybe I can find something for you to do.'

At the back of the house she dug in the can pile and found two old and battered aluminum saucepans. She carried them back and gave them to him. 'Here, maybe you can fix these.'

His manner changed. He became professional. 'Good as new I can fix them.' At the back of his wagon he set a little anvil, and out of an oily toolbox dug a small machine hammer. Elisa came through the gate to watch him while he pounded out the dents in the kettles. His mouth grew sure and knowing. At a difficult part of the work he sucked his underlip.

'You sleep right in the wagon?' Elisa asked.

'Right in the wagon, ma'am. Rain or shine I'm dry as a cow in there.'

'It must be nice,' she said. 'It must be very nice. I wish women could do such things.'

'It ain't the right kind of a life for a woman.'

Her upper lip raised a little, showing her teeth. 'How do you know? How can you tell?' she said.

'I don't know, ma'am,' he protested. 'Of course I don't know. Now here's your kettles, done. You don't have to buy no new ones.'

'How much?'

'Oh, fifty cents'll do. I keep my prices down and my work good. That's why I have all them satisfied customers up and down the highway.'

Elisa brought him a fifty-cent piece from the house and dropped it in his hand. 'You might be surprised to have a rival some time. I can sharpen scissors, too. And I can beat the dents out of little pots. I could show you what a woman might do.'

He put his hammer back in the oily box and shoved the little anvil out of sight. 'It would be a lonely life for a woman, ma'am, and a scary life, too, with animals creeping under the wagon all night.' He climbed over the singletree, steadying himself with a hand on the burro's white rump. He settled himself in the seat, picked up the lines. 'Thank you kindly, ma'am,' he said. 'I'll do like you told me; I'll go back and catch the Salinas road.'

'Mind,' she called, 'if you're long in getting there, keep the sand damp.'

'Sand, ma'am? . . . Sand? Oh, sure. You mean around the chrysantheums. Sure I will.' He clucked his tongue. The beasts leaned luxuriously into their collars. The mongrel dog took his place between the back wheels. The wagon turned and crawled out the entrance road and back the way it had come, along the river.

Elisa stood in front of her wire fence watching the slow progress of the caravan. Her shoulders were straight, her head thrown back, her eyes half-closed, so that the scene came vaguely into them. Her lips moved silently, forming the words 'Goodbye – goodbye.' Then she whispered, 'That's a bright direction. There's a glowing there.' The sound of her whisper startled her. She shook herself free and looked about to see whether anyone had been listening. Only the dogs had heard. They lifted their heads toward her from their sleeping in the dust, and then stretched out their chins and settled asleep again. Elisa turned and ran hurriedly into the house.

In the kitchen she reached behind the stove and felt the water tank. It was full of hot water from the noonday cooking. In the bathroom she tore off her soiled clothes and flung them into the corner. And then she scrubbed herself with a little block of pumice, legs and thighs, loins and chest and arms, until her skin was scratched and red. When she had dried herself she stood in front of a mirror in her bedroom and looked at her body. She tightened her stomach and threw out her chest. She turned and looked over her shoulder at her back.

After a while she began to dress, slowly. She put on her newest underclothing and her nicest stockings and the dress which was the symbol of her prettiness. She worked carefully on her hair, penciled her eyebrows and roughed her lips.

Before she was finished she heard the little thunder of hoofs and the shouts of Henry and his helper as they drove the red steers into the corral. She heard the gate bang shut and set herself for Henry's arrival.

His step sounded on the porch. He entered the house calling, 'Elisa, where are you?'

'In my room, dressing. I'm not ready. There's hot water for your bath. Hurry up. It's getting late.'

When she heard him splashing in the tub, Elisa laid his dark suit on the bed, and shirt and socks and tie beside it. She stood his polished shoes on the floor beside the bed. Then she went to the porch and sat primly and stiffly down. She looked toward the river road where the willow-line was still yellow with frosted leaves so that under the high grey fog they seemed a thin band of sunshine. This was the only color in the grey afternoon. She sat unmoving for a long time. Her eyes blinked rarely.

Henry came banging out of the door, shoving his tie inside his vest as he came. Elisa stiffened and her face grew tight. Henry stopped short and looked at her. 'Why – why, Elisa. You look so nice!'

'Nice? You think I look nice? What do you mean by "nice"?'

Henry blundered on. 'I don't know. I mean you look different, strong and happy.'

'I am strong? Yes, strong. What do you mean "strong"?'

He looked bewildered. 'You're playing some kind of a game,' he said helplessly. 'It's a kind of a play. You look strong enough to break a calf over your knee, happy enough to eat it like a watermelon.'

For a second she lost her rigidity. 'Henry! Don't talk like that. You didn't know what you said.' She grew complete again. 'I'm strong,' she boasted. 'I never knew before how strong.'

Henry looked down toward the tractor shed, and when he brought his eyes back to her, they were his own again. 'I'll get out the car. You can put on your coat while I'm starting.'

Elisa went into the house. She heard him drive to the gate and idle down his motor, and then she took a long time to put on her hat. She pulled it here and pressed it there. When Henry turned the motor off she slipped into her coat and went out.

The little roadster bounced along on the dirt road by the river, raising the birds and driving the rabbits into the brush. Two cranes flapped heavily over the willow-line and dropped into the riverbed.

Far ahead on the road Elisa saw a dark speck. She knew.

She tried not to look as they passed it, but her eyes would not obey. She whispered to herself sadly, 'He might have thrown them off the road. That wouldn't have been much trouble, not very much. But he kept the pot,' she explained. 'He had to keep the pot. That's why he couldn't get them off the road.'

The roadster turned a bend and she saw the caravan ahead. She swung full around toward her husband so she could not see the little covered wagon and the mismatched team as the car passed them.

In a moment it was over. The thing was done. She did not look back.

She said loudly, to be heard above the motor, 'It will be good, tonight, a good dinner.'

'Now you've changed again,' Henry complained. He took one hand from the wheel and patted her knee. 'I ought to take you in to dinner oftener. It would be good for both of us. We get so heavy out on the ranch.'

'Henry,' she asked, 'could we have wine at dinner?'

'Sure we could. Say! That will be fine.'

She was silent for a while; then she said, 'Henry, at those prize fights, do the men hurt each other very much?'

'Sometimes a little, not often. Why?'

'Well, I've read how they break noses, and blood runs down their chests. I've read how the fighting gloves get heavy and soggy with blood.'

He looked around at her. 'What's the matter, Elisa? I didn't know you read things like that.' He brought the car to a stop, then turned to the right over the Salinas River bridge.

'Do any women ever go to the fights?' she asked.

'Oh, sure, some. What's the matter, Elisa? Do you want to go? I don't think you'd like it, but I'll take you if you really want to go.'

She relaxed limply in the seat. 'Oh, no. No. I don't want to go. I'm sure I don't.' Her face was turned away from him. 'It will be enough if we can have wine. It will be plenty.' She turned up her coat collar so he could not see that she was crying weakly – like an old woman.